W9-AFY-573

On Christmas Eve

For Mrs. Dillon!

BY LIZ ROSENBERG • ILLUSTRATED BY JOHN CLAPP

Brookfield, Connecticut

2 0 0 3

A Neal Porter Book

Text copyright © 2002 by Liz Rosenberg

Illustrations copyright © 2002 by John Clapp

Published by Roaring Brook Press

A division of The Millbrook Press, 2 Old New Milford Road, Brookfield, Connecticut 06804

All rights reserved

Library of Congress Cataloging-in-Publication Data

Rosenberg, Liz.

On Christmas Eve / by Liz Rosenberg ; illustrated by John Clapp.

p.   cm.

Summary: Unable to reach Aunt Cleo's house on Christmas Eve because of a wild snowstorm, a young boy worries that Santa Claus

won't be able to find his family at the motel where they are stranded.

[1. Christmas—Fiction. 2. Santa Claus—Fiction. 3. Snow—Fiction.] I Clapp, John, ill. II. Title.

PZ7.R71894 On 2002

[E]—dc21   2002019951

ISBN 0-7613-1627-2 (trade)

2   4   6   8   10   9   7   5   3   1

ISBN 0-7613-2707-X (library binding)

2   4   6   8   10   9   7   5   3   1

Printed in Hong Kong

First edition

For David who makes it Christmas Eve every night
and for Claudia Jaccarino and her family
who loaned a little Jewish girl Christmas

—L.R.

For Mary—her first book.

—J.C.

It was a long drive to Aunt Cleo's house,
but that was all right.
It was Christmas Eve.

We crammed into the car.
My older brother, Adam, complained, and the baby blew bubbles.
I showed her the lit-up houses along the way.

It began to snow lightly as we crossed
the state line.
Then the storm grew thicker

and wilder.

My dad drove slower. A little slower still, his shoulders hunched over the wheel. Finally, Mom said, sighing, "We'll just have to stop somewhere for the night."

"But it's Christmas Eve," I said.

I looked over at my baby sister as if she was the one worrying about it. She blew another bubble.

One of the letters in the motel sign had gone out.
"They don't even have cable TV here! Or a
swimming pool!" yelled my brother.

Like we were going swimming in December.

But there was still this one thing. I mentioned it to my mother in a low voice. "There's no chimney—not even a mailbox."

"Santa will find us," my mother said. "He always finds a way."

"Only babies believe in Santa Claus," my brother told me later. We lay in the dark motel room. It didn't feel like Christmas.

All the same, after everyone else had fallen asleep, I hung up our stockings and laid out my last piece of Majic bubble gum and a package of peanut butter crackers. Just in case.

Then I waited by the motel room window.
"I wish Santa would come," I whispered.

The glass fogged with the breath of my
words. The fog formed a cloud, which grew
rounder, larger, silvery, and thin, then
disappeared into the air.

I must have fallen asleep.
Something woke me—what was it? The sound
came again, distant ringing, like frogs in summer.
In the sky I saw the faraway blinking lights of
an airplane. It had lights strung all over it, like a
Christmas tree.
No, it looked more like a strange sort of kite.

A sled!

He looked smaller than I had imagined. And the reindeer looked bigger.

He handed me the lighter of two
sacks. We tiptoed past the registration
desk and the humming ice machines.

"Thank you," he said.
"I love bubble gum."

I WISH SANTA WOULD

IF ONLY

WHY CANT WE

Back outside, he pointed to the sky.

MOTEL
VACANCY

Then, the reindeer lifted their heads. Swiftly and
surely they ran, till with a leap they bounded into
the air, then higher, flinging themselves at the sky
as if climbing a mountain—and flew, over the
broken motel sign

into Christmas morning.